ABOUT THE BANK STREET READY-TO-READ SERIES

Seventy years of educational research and innovative teaching have given the Bank Street College of Education the reputation as America's most trusted name in early childhood education.

Because no two children are exactly alike in their development, we have designed the *Bank Street Ready-to-Read* series in three levels to accommodate the individual stages of reading readiness of children ages four through eight.

- *Level 1:* GETTING READY TO READ—read-alouds for children who are taking their first steps toward reading.
- *Level 2:* READING TOGETHER—for children who are just beginning to read by themselves but may need a little help.
- *Level 3:* I CAN READ IT MYSELF—for children who can read independently.

Our three levels make it easy to select the books most appropriate for a child's development and enable him or her to grow with the series step by step. The *Bank Street Ready-to-Read* books also overlap and reinforce each other, further encouraging the reading process.

We feel that making reading fun and enjoyable is the single most important thing that you can do to help children become good readers. And we hope you'll be a part of Bank Street's long tradition of learning through sharing.

The Bank Street College of Education

LION AND LAMB
A Bantam Little Rooster Book
Simultaneous paper-over-board and trade paper editions/July 1989

Little Rooster is a trademark of Bantam Books,
a division of Bantam Doubleday Dell Publishing Group, Inc.

Series graphic design by Alex Jay/Studio J
Associate Editor: Randall Reich

Special thanks to James A. Levine, Betsy Gould, and
Erin B. Gathrid.

Library of Congress Cataloging-in-Publication Data
Hooks, William H.
Lion and lamb.

(Bank Street ready-to-read)
"A Byron Preiss Book."
"A Bantam little rooster book."
Summary: Lamb sees through the fierce reputation
of her friend Lion and recognizes him for
the gentle pussycat he really is.
[1. Lions—Fiction. 2. Sheep—Fiction. 3. Friendship—
Fiction] I. Brenner, Barbara. II. Degen, Bruce, ill.
III. Title. IV. Series.
PZ7.H7664Li 1989 [E] 88-7959
ISBN 0-553-05829-0
ISBN 0-553-34692-X (pbk.)

Published simultaneously in the United States and Canada

Bantam Books are published by Bantam Books, a division of Bantam Doubleday Dell Publishing Group, Inc. Its trademark, consisting of the words
"Bantam Books" and the portrayal of a rooster, is Registered in U.S. Patent
and Trademark Office and in other countries. Marca Registrada. Bantam
Books, 666 Fifth Avenue, New York, New York 10103.

PRINTED IN THE UNITED STATES OF AMERICA

WAK 0 9 8 7 6 5 4 3 2 1

Bank Street Ready-to-Read™

Lion and Lamb

by Barbara Brenner and William H. Hooks
Illustrated by Bruce Degen

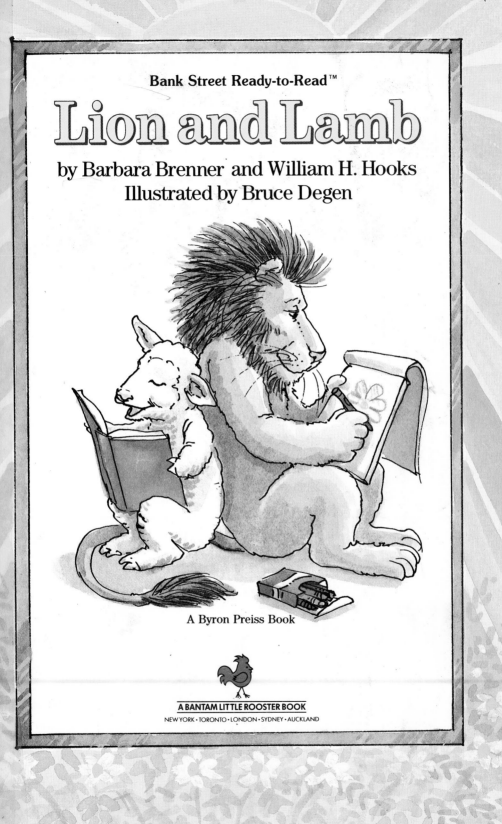

A Byron Preiss Book

A BANTAM LITTLE ROOSTER BOOK

NEW YORK · TORONTO · LONDON · SYDNEY · AUCKLAND

Contents

LION AND LAMB

Lamb was reading a book.
Lion was watching her.
"I can scare that lamb,"
Lion said to himself.

"ROAR!" he yelled.
Lamb didn't look up.
"ROAR! ROAR!"
Lamb still didn't look up.
"ROAR!" said Lion
as loudly as he could.

"Hush!" said Lamb.
"Not so loud!
Can't you see I'm reading?"

"You should be afraid
when a lion roars," said Lion.
"Why?" asked Lamb.
"Because a lion might bite."

"I might bite back," said Lamb.
"A lion could eat you," said Lion.
"Hush!" said Lamb.
"Go away. I'm busy."

Lion opened his mouth
and showed his teeth.
"Look, Lamb," he said.
"This is my scary face."

Lamb looked up from her book.
"Mmmm. Nice."
"Aren't you afraid of it?"
cried Lion.
"No. I like it," said Lamb.
"And I like you."

"But lambs must be afraid of lions."
"Not this lamb," said Lamb.
"Not even a little afraid?"
"No," said Lamb.
"Try," begged Lion.

"You can't fool me," said Lamb.
"You're really a pussycat."
Lion looked like he would cry.
"You won't tell, will you?"
he asked.

"Tell who?" asked Lamb.

"The other animals.

They don't know that I'm a pussycat."

"I won't tell," said Lamb.

"It will be our secret."

"Does that mean we're friends now?"
asked Lion.
"Now and forever," said Lamb.
"Now will you please let me
finish my book."

THE PARTY

Lion was looking sad.
"Today's the day," he said.
"It's my birthday."
"Oh, Lion! Happy Birthday!"
said Lamb.
"Thank you. But it's not happy."

"Birthdays should be happy,"
said Lamb.
"You should have a party."
"I can't," said Lion.
"Why not?" asked Lamb.
"No one will come.
Everyone is afraid I'll pounce."

"Will you pounce?" asked Lamb.
"Of course not. I never pounce.
But that's our secret."

"Don't worry, pussycat," said Lamb.
"Just come to my house at four o'clock."
Lamb blew Lion a kiss and skipped away.

Her first stop was Dog's house.
Dog was standing on the roof.
Lamb called up to him,
"Dog, can you come to a surprise party?"

"Who is it for?" he called back.
Lamb smiled sweetly.
"That's the surprise," she said.
"Then I'll come," said Dog.
"I love surprises."

Lamb hurried on to Pig's house.
Pig was sitting outside in the mud.
"Pig, can you come to a surprise party?"
Lamb asked.

"I can," said Pig.
"Who is going to be surprised?"
"You are," said Lamb.
"Come at three-thirty."

The next stop was Fox's house.
"Fox, there's a surprise party
at my house," she said.
"Will you come?"

"I will," said Fox.
"Who else is going to be there?"
"You'll be surprised!" said Lamb.

Lamb had one more stop to make.
At the store she bought a cake
and candles and paper hats.
Then she hurried home to get ready.

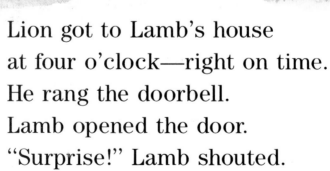

Lion got to Lamb's house
at four o'clock—right on time.
He rang the doorbell.
Lamb opened the door.
"Surprise!" Lamb shouted.

Lion stepped inside.

There were Dog and Pig and Fox.

They were wearing party hats.

And were they scared!

"This is a nice surprise," said Lion.
"Is it?" asked Dog.
"Lamb didn't tell us that
you were the surprise," said Pig.
"Are you going to pounce?" asked Fox.

"Lions never, never pounce
on their birthdays!" cried Lamb.
"And today is Lion's birthday.
So let's sing Happy Birthday.
Then we can cut the cake."

THE GHOST

Lion and Lamb were sitting
under a coconut tree
late one night.
They were making up stories.

"I like ghost stories," said Lamb.

"You do?" asked Lion.

"Yes, I do," said Lamb.

"I like very scary ones."

"Ghost stories are dumb," said Lion.

"Do they scare you?" asked Lamb.
"Lions don't scare," said Lion.
"Ghost stories scare me," said Lamb,
"but I still like them."
"They're dumb," said Lion again.
"If ghost stories don't scare you,
then I'll make one up," said Lamb.

"It happened late one night."
"Was it a dark night,
just like this?" asked Lion.
"It was on a dark and windy night,
just like this," said Lamb.
Lion tucked his tail under his feet.

"Two monkeys were sitting
under a tree," said Lamb.
"A tall coconut tree like this?"
asked Lion.
"Yes, just like this," said Lamb.

"The wind blew through the tree.
The monkeys heard a strange sound."
"What kind of sound?" asked Lion.
"A strange moaning sound," said Lamb.
"Like someone crying?" asked Lion.
"Yes," said Lamb.
Lion moved closer to Lamb.

"The two monkeys looked all around,"
said Lamb.
"They could not find anything.
The wind and the moaning grew louder.
It seemed to come closer and closer.
One monkey said, 'Let's run away!' "

"Smart monkey!" said Lion.
He moved a little closer to Lamb.
"The other monkey said, 'I think
we should stay right here.'"
"Dumb monkey," said Lion.

Lamb went on with her story.
"One monkey wanted to run—
but not alone.
One monkey wanted to stay—
but not alone.

The moaning sound seemed very close.
It was all around them.
'It's coming closer,' cried the monkey
who wanted to stay.
'It's right here,' cried the monkey
who wanted to run away.
The monkeys hugged each other
and shivered.''

Lion put his paw on Lamb's paw.
The wind shook the leaves
in the coconut tree.
"I can hear the moaning!" said Lion.
"It's right here!"

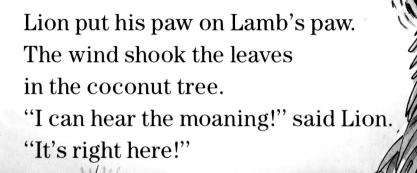

Lion jumped up so fast
that he knocked Lamb over.
Just then a great big coconut
blew out of the tree.
PLOP!
It fell right where Lamb was sitting.

"Oh, thank you," said Lamb.
"You pushed me away just in time.
You're some smart lion."
"I guess I am," said Lion.

"Now do you want to hear the rest
of the ghost story?" asked Lamb.
"No," said Lion.
"Ghost stories are dangerous."

Barbara Brenner is the author of more than thirty-five books for children, including *Wagon Wheels*, an ALA Notable Book. She writes frequently on subjects related to parenting and is co-author of *Choosing Books for Kids* and *Raising a Confident Child* in addition to being a Senior Editor for the Bank Street College Media Group. Ms. Brenner and her husband, illustrator Fred Brenner, have two sons. They live by a lake in Lords Valley, Pennsylvania.

William H. Hooks is the author of many books for children, including the highly acclaimed *Moss Gown*. He is also the Director of Publications at Bank Street College. As part of Bank Street's Media Group, he has been closely involved with such projects as the well-known Bank Street Readers and Discoveries: An Individualized Reading Program. Mr. Hooks lives with three cats in a Greenwich Village brownstone in New York City.

Bruce Degen has illustrated over twenty-five books for children, including the much-loved *Jessie Bear, What Will You Wear?*, *Jamberry*, *The Forgetful Bears Meet Mr. Memory*, and *The Magic School Bus at the Waterworks*, the illustrations for which were described as "hilarious" by the *New York Times Book Review*. Mr. Degen and his family live in New York City.